BATMAN!

By Billy Wrecks
Illustrated by Ethen Beavers

Batman created by Bob Kane

 A GOLDEN BOOK • NEW YORK

DC COMICS™

Copyright © 2013 DC Comics.
DC SUPER FRIENDS and all related characters and elements are trademarks of and © DC Comics.
WB SHIELD: ™ & © Warner Bros. Entertainment Inc.
(s13)

RHUS29797

Batman! originally published by Golden Books in 2012.
Superman! originally published by Golden Books in 2013.

randomhouse.com/kids

Educators and librarians, for a variety of teaching tools, visit us at
RHTeachersLibrarians.com

ISBN 978-0-375-97294-2

Printed in the United States of America

10 9 8 7 6 5 4 3 2 1

Superman, Green Lantern, Robin, and the Flash are the Super Friends. Together they are the world's greatest heroes. But only one hero is known as the Dark Knight of Gotham City—**Batman!**

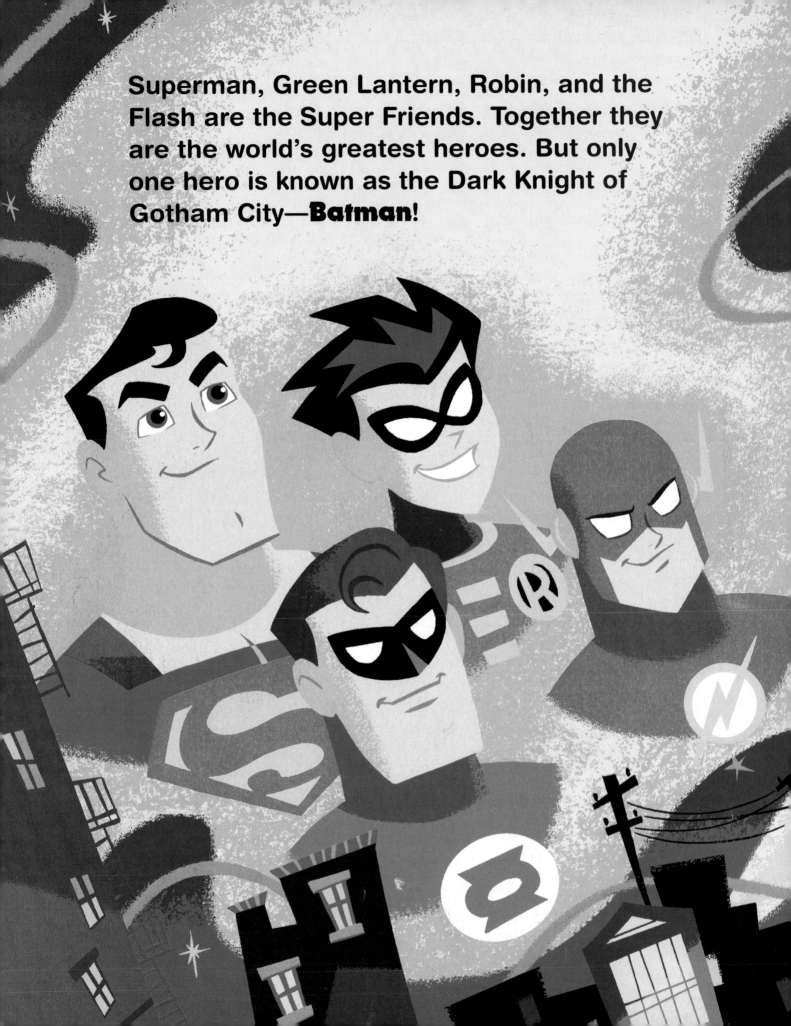

Batman doesn't have superpowers.
Instead, he uses his brains and
crime-fighting tools to catch crooks
and bring in the bad guys.

Batman trains hard to be extremely strong and fast! And he is a master of many different fighting styles.

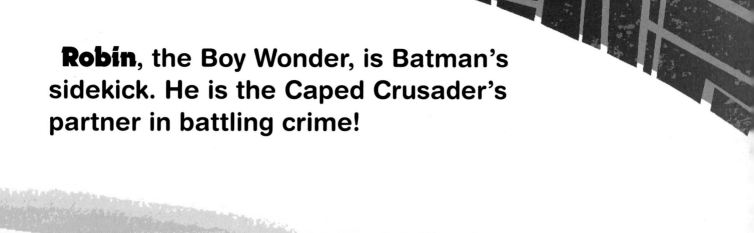

Robin, the Boy Wonder, is Batman's sidekick. He is the Caped Crusader's partner in battling crime!

Deep underground, Batman has a
high-tech lair called the **Batcave**.
Batman uses his Batcomputer and his
lab to study clues and solve crimes.

When the Bat-Signal shines in the sky, Batman knows there's trouble. That's when the Caped Crusader races into action with his rocket-powered **Batmobile**!

On water, the Dynamic Duo uses
the **Batboat** for high-speed chases.

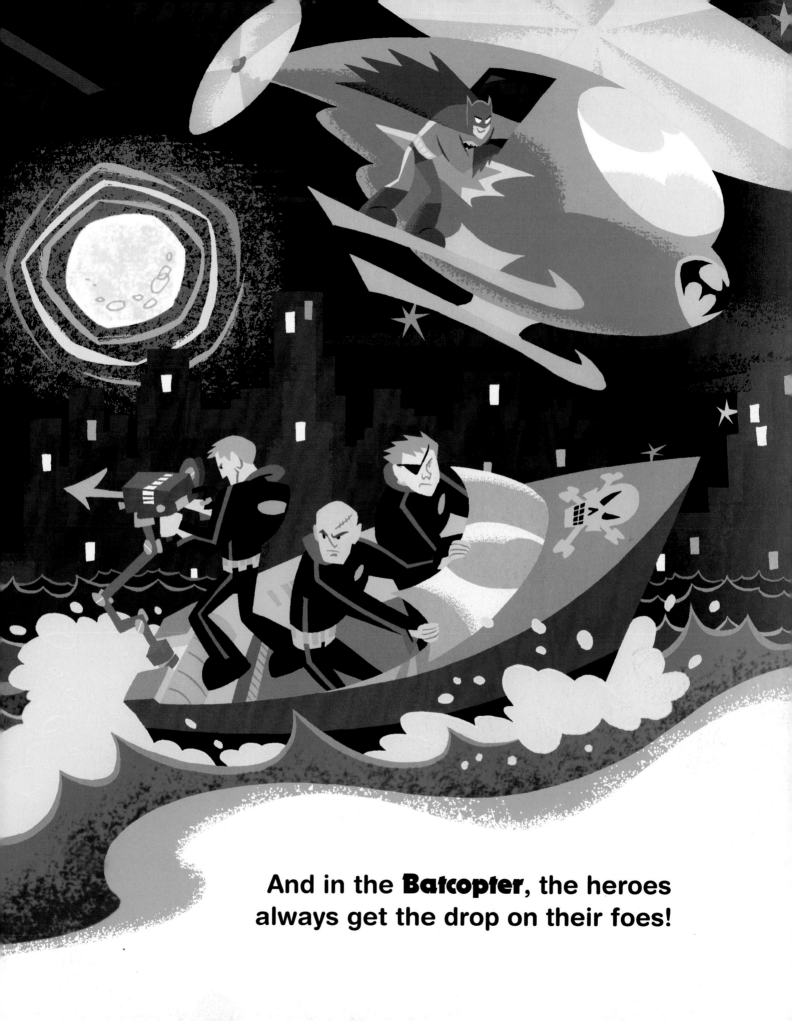

And in the **Batcopter**, the heroes always get the drop on their foes!

Batman and Robin wear Utility Belts packed with amazing crime-fighting gadgets, including **Batropes**, **Batarangs**, and **Bat-Cuffs!**

The Joker is Batman's greatest enemy. This criminal clown loves pulling pranks as much as committing crimes. Batman can never be sure what sort of terrible trouble the Joker will cause next!

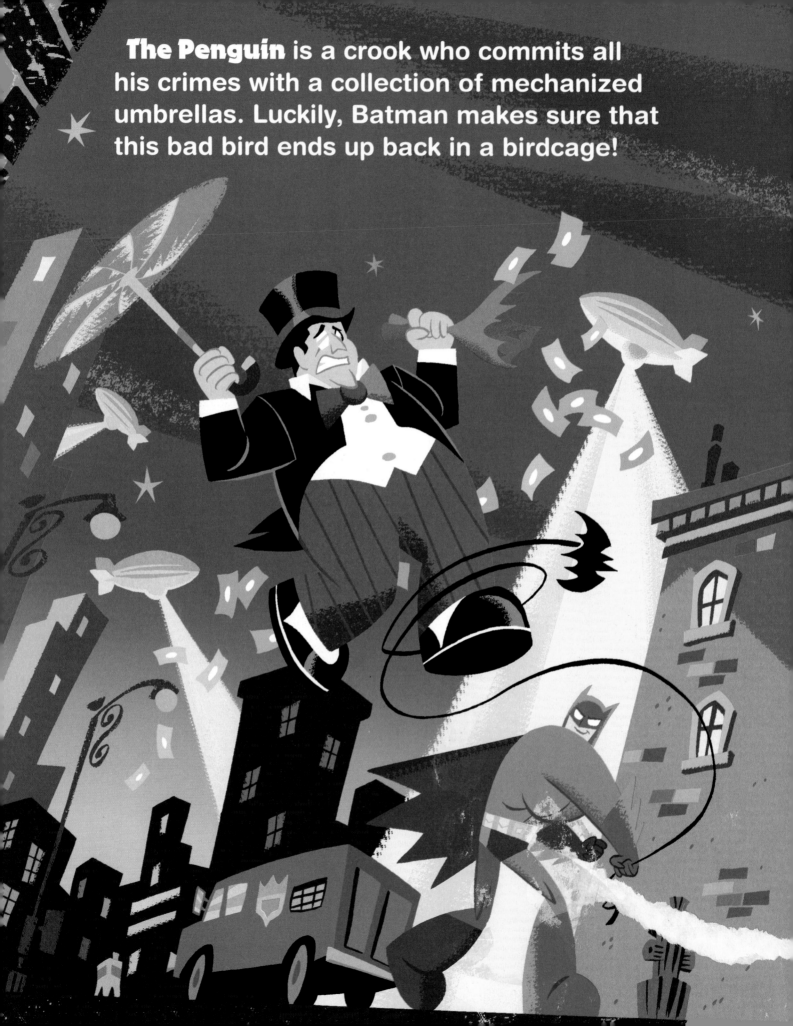

The Penguin is a crook who commits all his crimes with a collection of mechanized umbrellas. Luckily, Batman makes sure that this bad bird ends up back in a birdcage!

The **Riddler** gives Batman complicated clues to the crimes he is about to commit. But Batman always solves the Riddler's maddening puzzles in time to stop him!

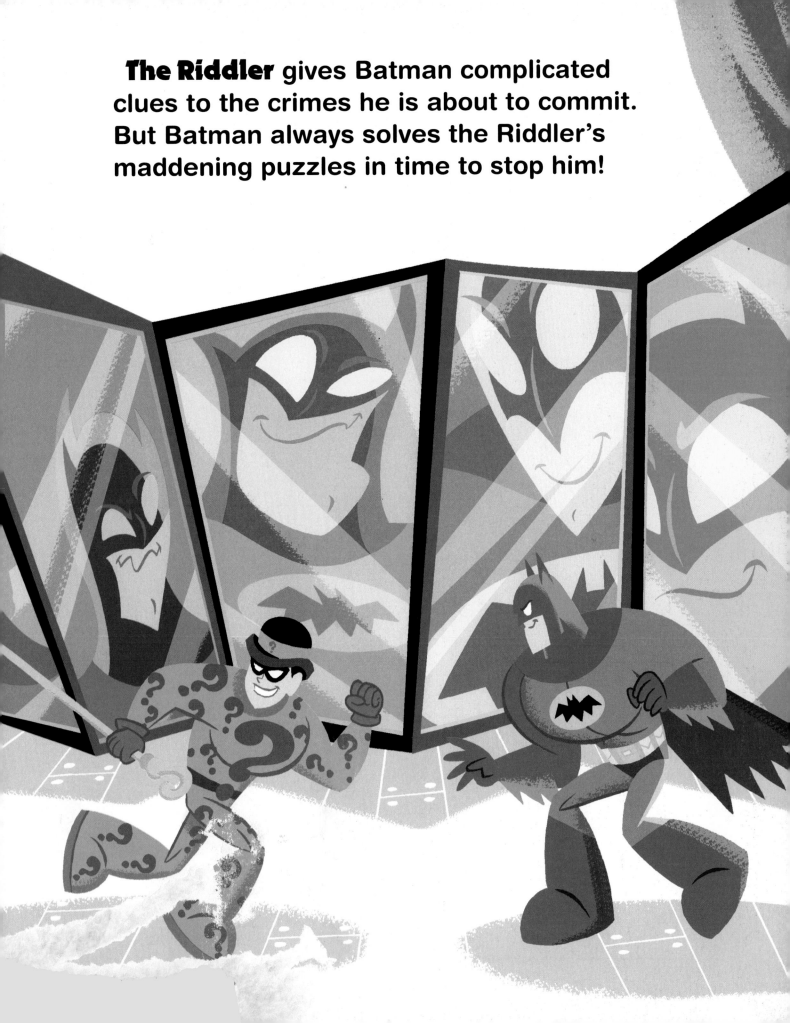

When powerful villains like **Lex Luthor** and the icy **Mr. Freeze** attack Gotham, the Super Friends help Batman put an end to their plans.

Batman and the Super Friends know that teamwork always saves the day—and helps put the bad guys away . . .

at least for a little while!

Thanks to Batman and the Super Friends, Gotham City—and the world—**stay safe!**

DC SUPER FRIENDS™

SUPERMAN!

By Billy Wrecks

Illustrated by Ethen Beavers

Superman created by Jerry Siegel and Joe Shuster

Superman is one of the mightiest heroes ever. Along with Batman, Green Lantern, and the rest of the Super Friends, Superman uses his amazing abilities to protect the world.

When aliens, natural disasters, monsters, and super-villains strike, the Super Friends are there to save the people of Earth!

Superman is actually from a planet called **Krypton**. When he was just a baby, his parents put him in a rocket and sent him to Earth—just as Krypton exploded!

Earth's yellow sun gives Superman many incredible **superpowers**. He can outrun the fastest express trains!

Superman is called the Man of Steel
because almost nothing can harm him.
He's **indestructible**!

Superman can **fly** at super-speed,
and he's **super-strong**.

Superman always arrives
just in time to save the day!

Superman's red-hot **heat vision** can cut through the hardest metals— or weld them back together!

And with his **freeze breath**, Superman can put out the hottest fires!

Whooooosh!

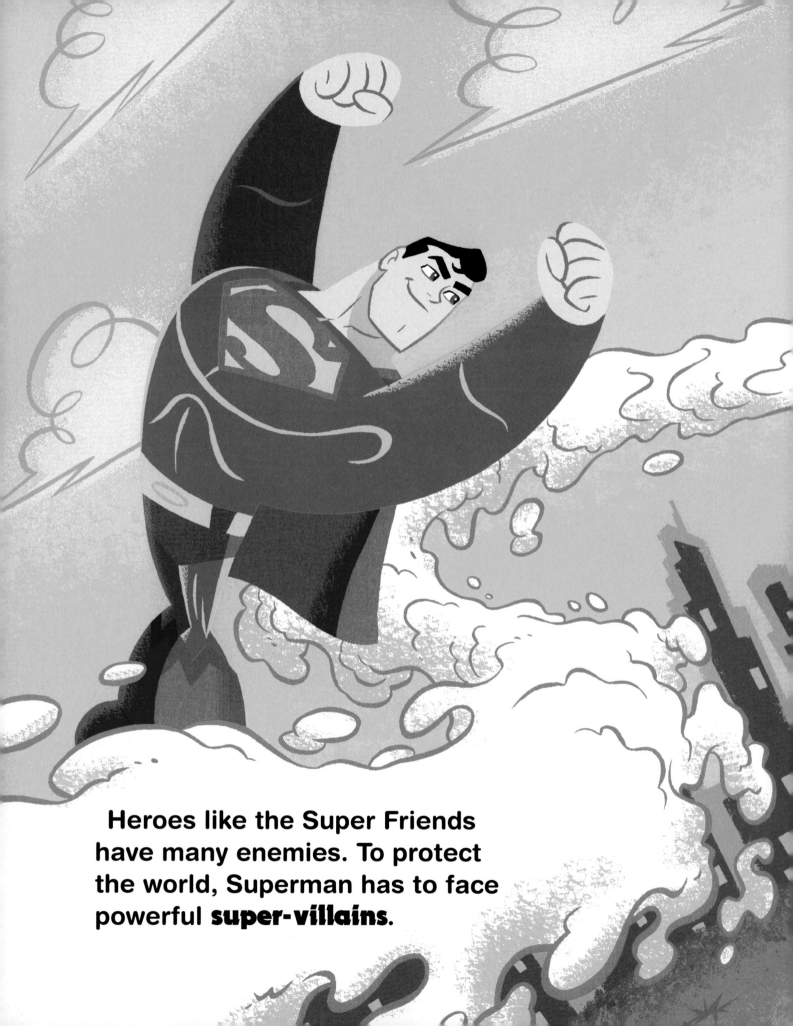

Heroes like the Super Friends have many enemies. To protect the world, Superman has to face powerful super-villains.

Lex Luthor is an evil super-genius who wants to destroy the Man of Steel. But Lex isn't smart enough to realize that Superman can get out of any sticky situation this villain dreams up!

General Zod is also from the planet Krypton. He has the same incredible powers as Superman.

But this vain villain is no match for Superman, who uses brains as well as brawn to stop Zod every time!

Brainiac travels from galaxy to galaxy, shrinking entire cities to put in his private library!

But even Brainiac's sophisticated science isn't enough to make Superman part of his collection.

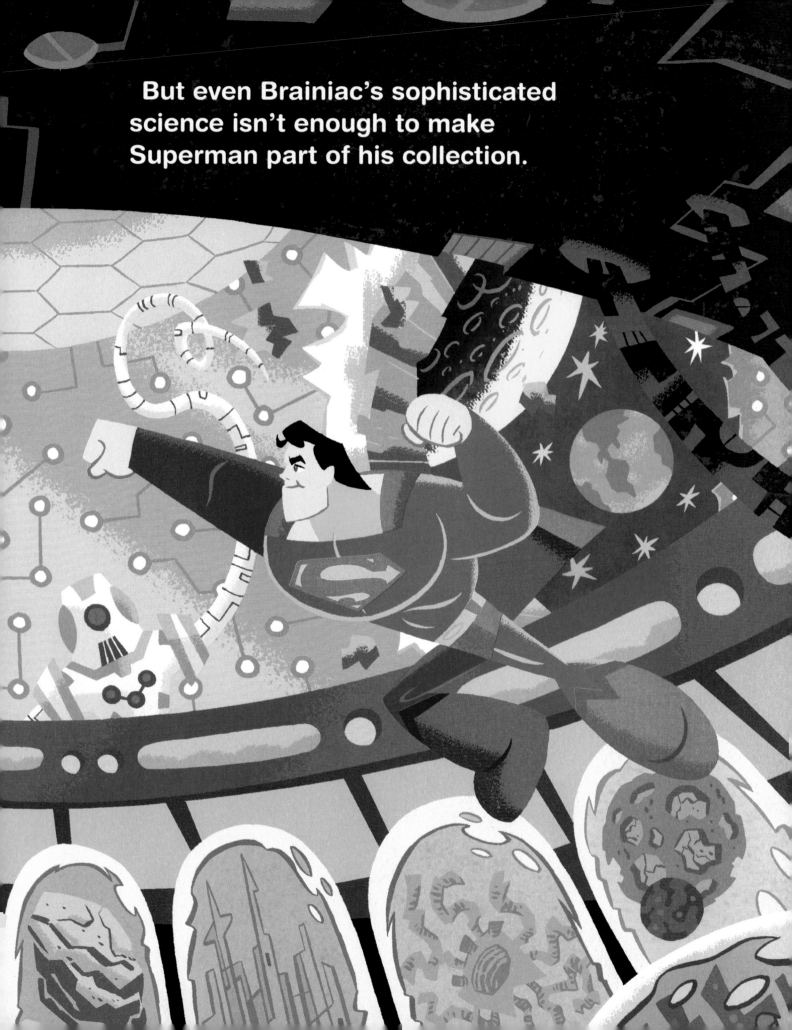

Superman and the Super Friends are always ready to defend Earth. With their combined abilities, there is no threat too big for them to handle. And there are some very **BIG** threats!

And when the world is safe again, Superman flies off, always ready for his next adventure.

"Up, up, and away!"